Banana spaghetti

Ann Cameron

Illustrated by Jamie Smith

Tamarind

BANANA SPAGHETTI
A TAMARIND BOOK 978 1 848 53086 7

First published in Great Britain in 1995 by Victor Gollancz, as part of
The Stories Huey Tells

This edition published by Tamarind Books,
an imprint of Random House Children's Publishers UK
A Random House Group Company

Tamarind edition published 2014

1 3 5 7 9 10 8 6 4 2

Text copyright © Ann Cameron, 1995
Cover and interior illustrations copyright © Jamie Smith, 2014

The right of Ann Cameron and Jamie Smith to be identified as the author and
illustrator of this work has been asserted in accordance with the
Copyright, Designs and Patents Act 1988.

The Random House Group Limited supports the Forest Stewardship Council® (FSC®),
the leading international forest-certification organisation. Our books carrying the FSC
label are printed on FSC®-certified paper. FSC is the only forest-certification scheme
supported by the leading environmental organisations, including Greenpeace. Our paper
procurement policy can be found at www.randomhouse.co.uk/environment.

Tamarind Books are published by Random House Children's Publishers UK,
61–63 Uxbridge Road, London W5 5SA

www.**tamarindbooks**.co.uk
www.**randomhousechildrens**.co.uk
www.**randomhouse**.co.uk

Addresses for companies within The Random House Group Limited can be found at:
www.randomhouse.co.uk/offices.htm

THE RANDOM HOUSE GROUP Limited Reg. No. 954009

A CIP catalogue record for this book is available from the British Library.

Printed and bound in Great Britain by CPI Group (UK), Croydon, CR0 4YY

To Bill Cherry

Contents

Blue Light, Green Light

My brother Julian isn't scared of the dark. Night-time doesn't bother him. He just gets into bed, puts a pillow over his head, and goes to sleep.

Not me. I don't like the dark, and I get scary dreams. One I dreamed lots of times, and every time I dreamed it, it got worse. Finally I told it to Julian.

"I was walking in a high place. Then all of a sudden I went over a cliff. The whole world just dissolved. I was falling straight down to the bottom of the universe. I was going to hit it and die."

"Then what?" Julian asked.

"I woke up."

"That's nothing!" Julian said. "I've had much scarier dreams than that! Once I dreamed a lion licked my face. But I wasn't even scared!"

"A lion is not like falling!" I said. He made me angry. He always acts like nothing I say is important.

"It's no use telling you anything!" I said.

I told my mum my dream, how when I was falling it was like my stomach climbed up into my head.

She said maybe the dream wouldn't happen any more if my body had more calcium. She said she'd make me warm milk with honey before I went to bed.

I told my dad my dream.

"I was falling through nowhere," I said. "There wasn't one solid thing anywhere! And I just kept dropping faster and faster all the way to the bottom of the universe."

"Huey," my dad said, "the universe doesn't have a bottom. So you can't hit it. And there isn't any nowhere! Every place is somewhere."

"In the dream, it's like I'm paralysed.

4

And it seems like I'm nowhere."

"Maybe your mattress is too soft," my dad said. "I'll put a piece of plywood under it."

And he did. But the next night, even with calcium and plywood, I was falling just the same.

"Plywood didn't mend it," I told my dad. "I still feel like I'm falling in nowhere."

He had just come home from work. "Give me time to think," he said.

He went into the house and sat in his favourite chair. He put his elbows on his knees and his chin in his hands. He shut his eyes and pulled his hair. He sighed.

Then he opened his eyes and smiled.

"I have just what you need in the cellar!" he said.

He ran down the cellar stairs and came up with something in a bag.

"Come on!" he said.

We went straight upstairs to my bed.

He reached into the bag like a magician.

"This is the answer!" he said.

He pulled out a brand-new brick.

"How is that going to help me?" I asked.

"Feel it!" Dad said.

I felt it.

"This brick," my dad said, "is solid."

He set it down in the middle of my bed.

"Now," he said, "try it."

"Try it?" I said.

"Yes," he said. "Lie down on it!"

"Lie down on it?" I said.

"Yes!" he said.

I didn't really want to try it, but I did.

I lay back. I could feel the edges of the brick against my spine. I could even feel the three round holes in the middle of it. I sat up.

"How did it feel, Huey?" my dad asked.

"Hard!" I said.

8

"See!" my dad said. "That's how the world really is. Hard! Full of hard stuff. You really can't just fall away to nowhere. If you sleep on this nice new brick, it will tell your body that!"

"Dad," I said, "if I lie on that brick I will never sleep again!"

My dad looked disappointed.

"Anyhow," he said, "maybe your body will remember how it felt and not forget the world is solid. Or, if you wake up, maybe just touching it will help," he said. He put it next to the lamp on my night table.

"What's that?" Julian asked when he saw it.

"It's a present from Dad," I said.

"Why didn't he give me a present?" Julian asked.

"You don't need one," I said.

And when I woke up at night, I touched

the brick. It made me feel better, but it didn't stop my bad dream.

Julian and I have a friend, Gloria. I was scared to tell her about my dream. I was scared she'd make me feel small, like Julian. But one day when Julian wasn't around I told her anyway.

"That's a horrible dream!" she said. She sounded like she really understood how it was. Even though she was understanding a horrible thing, her understanding made me feel good.

"Do you get scary dreams?" I asked.

"Sometimes," she said. "Really bad ones."

And she told me about them.

The worst was about some bad guys with guns trying to break down the door to her house. She and her mum and dad pushed and pushed against the door to hold the bad guys back. And then the

door broke, and she and her parents started running.

But they couldn't run fast enough . . .

"That dream is as bad as mine!" I said.

"Yes!" Gloria said. "And when I wake up, I feel scared and kind of sick to my stomach. And I don't want to go back to sleep. I can be brave when I'm awake – but it's hard to be brave when you're asleep."

"I wish we could signal to each other

when we wake up at night," I said. "That way we could tell each other that we are OK."

"With lights in our bedroom windows, we could do it," Gloria said. "I could see  yours shining, and you could see mine."

"We should do it," I said.

So we asked our parents for permission to buy lights and hang them in our windows. Gloria's parents said she could do it if I could. My parents said I had to ask Julian.

I thought he would say no. But he didn't. He said it was a good idea.

My dad drove us to a hardware shop. We bought reflector lights with strong clamps and coloured reflector bulbs.

Gloria bought a green bulb. Julian and I bought a blue one.

My dad let the three of us out of the truck at Gloria's house. The clamp on the light was hard to open. Gloria's mum and dad clamped it to the windowsill for her. Gloria screwed in the bulb and plugged in the light. It worked!

At our house we got the light set up just like Gloria's, and Gloria stayed for supper. Afterwards she went home so we could test our signals.

Julian and I went up to our room. Exactly at nine, we screwed in the bulb. Our blue light shone out. Down the street there came an answer – a green light glowing in Gloria's window.

"It works!" Julian said. "And it isn't quite so dark in here. Sometimes it gets too dark. That's why I sleep with a pillow over my head."

I was surprised. "I thought you liked the dark," I said.

"A whole lot of it is too much," Julian said.

I thought. Maybe it wasn't just me and Gloria that didn't like the dark. Maybe it scares everybody a little.

"If it gets too dark," I told him, "you can come and get in bed with me sometimes."

And now, sometimes, he does.

There's one good thing about the dark. In daylight our signals don't show up. It's the dark that makes them beautiful.

I don't have falling dreams any more. I don't know why. Maybe the reason is the plywood. Maybe it's my brick. Maybe it's hot milk with honey. Maybe it's because I know everybody is scared sometimes.

Now when I wake up at night, there's a blue glow in our room. I know our light is shining strong to Gloria's house.

I get up and go to the window. Beyond lots of dark houses I see Gloria's green light. It is steady and bright, like a beam from a lighthouse that guides ships away from danger.

I stand a long time at the window looking out, feeling happy.

We are OK. Me, and Julian, and Gloria.

The Rule

My mum and dad have a rule. At every meal, Julian and I have to eat at least a little bit of everything on our plates.

Julian doesn't mind. My mum says that ever since he was a baby he liked to eat every single vegetable and all kinds of strange foods.

When I was born, my mum thought that I would be like Julian. I'm not. It's because of me that they made up the rule.

Because of the rule, I have eaten a little bit of oysters and asparagus. I have eaten a little bit of aubergine and turnips.

I have eaten a piece of radish so tiny that afterwards I had to use a magnifying glass to show my parents there was something missing from that radish.

Because of the radish, they added to the rule. You cannot use a magnifying glass to prove you tasted something. You have to eat more of it than that.

There is one other part to the rule. It is about restaurants. That part is:

Food in restaurants is expensive. In a restaurant, if you order something, you better eat it all.

One day my mum and dad decided to take me and Julian out for dinner. They invited Gloria to come too.

My mum told us to dress up for the restaurant, with dark trousers and white shirts and our best Sunday shoes. Julian tried to dress to look grown up. I was worried about the rule. I tried to dress the best way for getting hungry. I fastened the belt on my trousers very tight. I hoped that would make me hungry.

We stopped and picked up Gloria, who

was all dressed up too. She had on a pink dress and new shoes with bows on them.

The name of the restaurant was King Henry's. There were lots of cars parked in the front, and there was a red carpet leading inside. A man as dressed up as us opened the door and took us to a table.

He was very tall and thin. He looked like he could eat ten dinners at once and they would just disappear inside him. He probably knew the right way to wear his belt for getting hungry.

When he brought us menus, I twisted my neck around so I could see his belt. It was very loose! I loosened mine three notches. Right away I felt hungry.

The menu was in a leather holder. It was very big, with fancy gold and black writing. I looked for words I knew. A little card was pinned right in the middle of the first page:

Special

Grilled Giant Forest Mushrooms with Fresh Trout from cold mountain rivers

"Special" is my favourite word. I also like the words "giant", "fresh" and "river". The words made me very hungry. I loosened my belt one more notch.

"What's trout?" I asked my mum.

"It's a fish," she said.

"That's what I want," I said.

"Are you sure?" my dad asked. "Are you sure you don't want a hamburger? That's what Julian's having. Or maybe you'd like the chef's salad? That's what Gloria's having."

"I'm sure," I said. "I want the Special."

"You know you'll have to eat it when it comes," my mum said.

"I will," I said.

The thin man brought Julian's hamburger, Gloria's salad, and my mum and dad's chicken. He brought me the Special.

The giant mushrooms were all around the plate, just like a forest. The trout was in the middle. He still wore his skin and his head. His mouth was open as if he was gasping for air. His eye was big and white and sad and cooked. It looked straight at me.

"Sorry," I said. I looked away.

I looked at the giant mushrooms. Their tops were like wings. They looked like a dark forest. They were a little mushy, but they still looked like rooms. Probably

elves had lived under them and danced
around them in the moonlight. If I ate
one, I could be eating an elf's house.

But I had to do it. "Sorry," I said.

I took my knife and fork. I cut myself a
bite. It tasted like a buttered forest. I liked
the taste. I ate all my mushrooms.

"Huey ate all his mushrooms!" my
mum said.

"But," my dad said, "he hasn't touched
his fish."

23

"I will," I said.

I didn't want to touch it with my finger. I touched the tail with my knife.

The eye of the fish looked at me. I stopped touching its tail.

I wondered if I was supposed to eat the eye. If I had to, I would eat the tail first. I would save the eye till last.

I could eat the fish if I didn't look at it.

But it is hard to eat your food if you don't look at it. You keep missing the plate with your fork.

There were mirrors on two sides of the room. I could see my fork miss the plate two ways. I could see the heaps of salad left on Gloria's plate.

"Mrs Bates," Gloria said, "do you mind if I don't eat all my salad?"

"Of course not, honey," my mum said. "You're a guest."

I turned around in my chair and looked

at the back of the room. There was an aquarium! It was full of purple fish, live ones with frilly tails like ballerinas' dresses. They were watching me. It looked like they were talking to each other. They wanted to see what I would do.

"Sorry," I muttered to the purple fish. I put my fork in my lap.

"Huey," my dad said, "We're almost done."

"Sorry," I said.

"You don't have to eat the head or the tail or the skin," my mum explained. "Just break the skin open and eat the flesh."

"Flesh!" I said.

"Meat," my mum said.

"Huey – if you finish your fish, you can have ice cream," my dad promised.

I moved my legs. My fork slipped out of my lap and so did my napkin. Right away the thin man saw. He picked them up and took them away. Then he put a clean fork by my plate. He handed me a fresh napkin.

I remembered something I saw once on TV – a live heart operation. The doctors didn't look at the patient. They kept him covered up with a cloth. My mum said they did it so they could forget he was a person and cut.

I took my fresh napkin and threw it

over my whole fish, all but the middle.

Julian almost choked on a piece of bread. "Huey's napkin!" he said, pointing.

"Yuck!" Gloria said.

"Huey!" my dad exclaimed.

"Your manners!" my mum reminded.

I didn't listen. There wasn't time.

I picked up my fork. I took a big chunk out of my fish's side, and chewed it, and swallowed it.

I swallowed three times extra for safety. I ate nine more big bites.

"Huey ate almost all of it," Gloria said.

"Huey has to eat it all," Julian said. "That's the rule!"

I looked at Mum and Dad. "Do I have to?" I said. I felt awfully full.

"Julian," my mum said, "rules aren't absolute.

People make rules to make life better. If a rule doesn't work, it can be changed."

My dad said, "Huey ate lots of good food tonight. If he ate more, he might burst."

My mum said, "I'm proud of Huey. He ate two new foods. He was adventurous."

It sounded like I was a hero. An explorer maybe.

"But what about the rule?" Julian protested.

"Maybe we don't even need it any more," my mum said. "What do you think, Huey?"

I looked at my plate. The mushrooms were all gone. I'd eaten almost all the fish. Julian never ever ate that much. If he ever tried it in a restaurant, he could never do it.

"Let's keep the rule," I said.

Chef Huey

"Food should be different from the way it is," I said to my mum. "Then I wouldn't mind eating it."

"How should it be different?" my mum asked.

"I don't exactly know," I said.

"Maybe you will work it out and be a chef," my mum said.

"What's a chef?" I asked.

"A chef is a very good cook who sometimes invents new things to eat," my mum told me.

The next day we went to the supermarket. I saw pictures of chefs on some of the food packages. They were all smiling. I wondered if when they were little they had to eat what their parents told them to eat. Maybe that's why they became chefs – so they could invent foods that they liked to eat. Probably that's when they became happy.

The chef with the biggest smile of all was Chef Marco on the tin of Chef Marco's Spaghetti.

"Please get that tin," I said to my mum. "I want to take it home."

I wanted to invent something with it, but I wasn't sure what.

At first I couldn't think of anything it went with. Instead, I thought of cakes like pillows. I thought of carrots that would be fastened together around meat loaf to make skyscrapers on our plates. One night I did tie some carrots around a meat loaf my dad made – but the strings that fastened them came loose in the oven, and the skyscraper fell down.

It was the night before Mother's Day when I thought of a brand-new food.

I could see it in my mind. Something yellow. A happy, yellow food. One that didn't mind being eaten.

In the morning, Julian and I were going to bring my mum breakfast in bed. Julian was going to fry eggs. I told him I had a better idea.

"What is it?" he asked.

"Banana spaghetti," I said.

"Banana spaghetti?" he said. "I've never heard of it!"

"It's a new invention!" I said. "It will

be a one hundred percent surprise."

Julian likes surprises. "So how do we make it?" he asked.

"Simple!" I said. "We have bananas and we have spaghetti. All we have to do is put them together."

Julian thought about it. "We'd better get up early tomorrow," he said. "Just in case."

At six a.m. we went downstairs very quietly and turned on the lights in the kitchen. We went to work.

We mashed up three ripe bananas. I took out the tin of Chef Marco's Spaghetti. In the picture on the tin, Chef Marco had his arms spread out wide, with a steaming platter balanced above his head on one hand.

I decided to stand that way when I brought Mum the banana spaghetti. I would go up the stairs ahead of Julian

with her plate, so Julian couldn't take all the credit.

I held the tin and Julian opened it. We put the spaghetti in a bowl. It had a lot of tomato sauce on it – the colour of blood.

"We have to get the tomato off!" I said.

We put the spaghetti in the sink and washed it with hot water. It got nice and clean. We put it on a plate.

"It looks kind of spongy," Julian said.

"It will be good," I said. "We just need to put the sauce on it."

Julian dumped all the mashed banana on the top.

"Banana spaghetti!" I said.

"Taste it!" Julian said.

But I wasn't sure I wanted to.

"You try it!" I said.

Julian tasted it. His lips puckered up. He wiped his mouth with a kitchen towel.

"It will be better when it's hot," he said.

We put it in a pan on the stove and it got hot. Very hot. The banana scorched. It smelled like burning rubber.

Julian turned off the stove. We looked into the pan.

"Not all of it burned," Julian said. "Just the bottom. We can put the rest on the plates."

We did. Then we looked at it.

Banana spaghetti was not the way I

had imagined it. It wasn't yellow. It was brown. It wasn't happy. It looked miserable.

It looked worse than turnips, worse than aubergine, worse than a baked fish eye.

"Maybe it's better than we think," Julian said. "When you don't like some stuff, Mum always tells you it's better than you think."

"Will she eat it?" I asked.

"She'll eat it because we made it," Julian said.

"That might not be a good enough reason," I said.

"You can tell her just to try a little bit," Julian advised.

That seemed like a good idea. "Let's take it upstairs," I said. I handed Mum's plate to him.

"No," Julian said, "you take it up. It's your invention." He handed the plate back to me.

I put the plate on a tray with a knife and a fork and a napkin. I started up the stairs. I tried holding the tray above my head on one hand, but it was very tippy. I couldn't do it the way Chef Marco did. And I wasn't happy like Chef Marco, either. I wished Julian was with me.

I climbed five steps. It's better than you think, I told myself.

On the sixth step I just sat down with the tray in my lap, and stayed there.

I heard the door to my parents' room open. I heard feet hurrying down the stairs. My dad's.

He stopped when he saw me.

"Huey," he said, "what are you doing?"

"Thinking," I said. "What are you doing?"

"Going for coffee — what is that stuff you're holding?"

"It's banana spaghetti," I said. "I invented it. Julian and I made it for Mum. We thought it would be good. But it didn't come out the way I wanted it to."

 My dad sat by me and looked at it. I passed it to him.

"It does seem to have a problem," he said. "Maybe several problems."

He sniffed it and wrinkled his nose. He got a faraway, professional look on his face, as if he was comparing it with all the banana foods he had ever tasted in his life. He looked as wise as Chef Marco.

"Banana spaghetti," he said. "It's a good idea. You just need to make it differently."

"How?"

"Spaghetti is usually made with flour and eggs," Dad explained. "But I think we could make it from flour and banana. After I have my coffee, we can try."

38

We went to the kitchen. Julian had the eggs out. He was getting a frying pan.

"You can put the frying pan away, Julian," my dad said. "We're making banana spaghetti."

He flicked the switch on the coffee maker. In a minute coffee spurted out, and he poured himself a cup and sipped it.

"I'm ready," he said. "Peel me three bananas, boys!"

We did.

"Now put them in this bowl and mash them!" he said.

We did. They came out sort of white, just like the first ones we mashed. And flour wasn't going to change the colour.

"Dad," I said. "I want banana spaghetti to be yellow. It's not going to be yellow, is it?"

"Not without help," my dad said. "Look in the cupboard. Maybe there's

some yellow food colouring in there."

We took everything out of the cupboard. Toothpicks, napkins, salt, burn ointment, tins of soup, instant coffee, six pennies, and a spider's web. At the very back I found a tiny bottle of yellow stuff. I showed it to my dad.

"That's it!" he said. "Put some in, Huey! Just a few drops."

I did.

"Stir that yellow around," he said.

We took spoons and did it.

"Bring me the flour," he said.

We did.

He dumped some in the bowl.

"This is hard to mix," my dad said, "so let me do it."

With a fork he mixed the flour and banana into a dough.

"Julian! Spread some flour on this counter!" he said.

Julian did.

My dad set the dough on the floured counter. "I have to knead this dough," he said. "You boys clean the cupboard and put everything back in it."

We did, except for the pennies. We asked if we could have them, and my dad

said yes. We put them in our pockets.

Dad rolled up the sleeves of his pyjamas and pushed the dough back and forth under his hands, twisting and turning and pressing it hard, until it was smooth and not sticky.

"The dough has to rest so it will be stretchy," he said. He covered it with an upside-down bowl and put a big pot of water on the stove to boil.

"What should go in the sauce?" he asked. "It's your invention, Huey, so you decide."

I tried to think of the best ingredient in the world.

"What about – whipped cream?" I asked. I never had any spaghetti that way, but I thought it would be good.

"Whipped cream! A great idea!" my dad said.

I poured cream into a bowl. Dad got the electric mixer out, and I beat the cream.

"How about – sugar?" Julian said.

"Sugar is right," I said. Julian poured some in.

"Now," Dad said, "what about spices? How about – oregano?" And he gave me the oregano bottle so I could smell it.

It smelled like pizza. "No!" I said.

"How about – cinnamon?" he asked.

Julian and I both smelled the cinnamon. "Yes!" we said.

"And how about – ginger?" He handed me the jar.

Julian and I both smelled it. Julian said no. I said yes. Banana spaghetti is mine, so I won. My dad shook in some ginger, and then he beat the cream till it was thick and fluffy.

"How about – sliced banana?" Julian said.

I said yes. We sliced a banana. My dad stirred it into the cream.

We all tasted the sauce. It was delicious.

"Now," my dad said, "the spaghetti."

He uncovered the spaghetti dough and asked us for the rolling pin and the flour.

He rolled the dough, and then we rolled

it some more. Finally, when it was thin and stretched out like a blanket, he folded it over twice and cut it into strips.

Julian and I separated the strips and unfolded them. They were long and smooth and yellow. We held them in our hands gently, like Christmas tree tinsel.

The water in the pot was boiling as if it wanted to jump out. We stood on chairs by the stove and dropped in all the spaghetti strings at once. They sank and swam in the pot for just a minute before my dad dipped in a fork and fished one out.

He tasted it.

"Done!" he said. "Quick! Get the plates ready!"

We did. Dad set a strainer in the sink. He poured everything out of the pot. All the water washed down the drain. The spaghetti stayed in the strainer. He divided the spaghetti on the plates and shook some cinnamon over it. I spread the sauce on top. It looked good – except for one thing.

"Just a minute!" I said. I found a bag of chopped peanuts and tossed some on top of each plate of banana spaghetti.

"Is that everything, Huey?" my dad asked.

"Yes," I said.

"Delivery time!" Julian said.

I went first with two plates. Julian came behind me with the other two plates. My dad came last, with silverware, coffee and orange juice on a tray.

My hands were full. I knocked on the bedroom door with the edge of one plate.

"Come in!" my mum said. I hoped she would be just waking, but she was sitting up in bed, reading a book. She looked hungry.

I set one plate on the dressing table. I

brought the other to her the way Chef Marco would have done it, held out like a gift.

"Happy Mother's Day!" I said.

"What is this?" she said.

"Just – banana spaghetti," I said.

My dad handed her a fork. She tasted it.

"Delicious!" she said. "Very strange, but very delicious."

"Dad and Julian helped me," I said. "But it's my invention."

We arranged everything so we could all eat on the bed. When we had eaten all the spaghetti, we had second helpings of the sauce.

My mum scooped up the last bit of her sauce with a spoon. "Banana spaghetti! What a wonderful breakfast!" she said.

And I was very proud. Just yesterday there was no such thing as banana spaghetti in the whole world – and now

there is. Just like once the telephone didn't exist, or television, or space stations. A lot of people believed those things could never exist. But then some great inventor made them.

I am an inventor. And a chef.

And I know what I want for dinner on my birthday. Banana spaghetti. With chocolate shavings over the sauce, and seven yellow candles on top.

About the Author

Ann Cameron has worked in publishing and as a university teacher. Her most adventurous experience was working with archaeologists on a Mayan dig in the rainforest of Belize. She washed pieces of ancient pottery and cooked for the camp. At night she slept in a hammock in an open-air hut, while around her boa constrictors climbed up to the thatched roof to hunt mice.

After spending many years in New York and Guatemala, Central America, she now lives in Portland, Oregon, USA. She is the author of seventeen books, including the timeless series of stories featuring brothers Julian and Huey, and she has been a finalist for the U.S. National Book Award for Young People's Literature. Please visit **anncameronbooks.com** for further information about Ann and her books.

Dad's Really Difficult Quiz

1. What does Huey dream about?

2. What object does Dad leave on Huey's night table?

3. What colour bulb does Gloria buy?

4. What does Huey order at the restaurant?

5. What is the name of the chef on the spaghetti tin?

Turn to the back of the book to see the answers!

Julian's Wonderful Wordsearch

Ten words are hidden in the wordsearch.
Can you find them all?

1. Banana
2. Spaghetti
3. Sugar
4. Flour
5. Cinnamon

6. Cream
7. Ginger
8. Dough
9. Peanuts
10. Mixer

B	I	C	G	Q	D	H	J	K	A	X
A	C	I	R	M	L	O	F	P	Z	B
N	B	N	F	E	J	W	U	L	H	F
A	Q	N	H	C	A	Y	E	G	I	L
N	D	A	Y	F	Z	M	B	K	H	O
A	Z	M	I	X	E	R	T	U	P	U
I	D	O	V	H	G	I	N	G	E	R
G	E	N	A	M	T	S	F	J	K	X
Z	H	S	U	G	A	R	B	H	W	T
B	Y	W	I	P	E	A	N	U	T	S
S	P	A	G	H	E	T	T	I	E	D

Turn to the back of the book to see the answers!

Huey's Hilarious Jokes

Q. Why is a trout easy to weigh?

A. Because it has its own scales!

Q. What do you call a fish with no eyes?

A. Fsh!

Q. Why are fish so smart?

A. Because they are always in schools!

Q. What fish can go up the river at 100 miles per hour?

A. A motor pike!

Answers

Dad's Really Difficult Quiz:

1) Falling; 2) A brick; 3) Green;
4) Trout; 5) Chef Marco

Julian's Wonderful Wordsearch:

B	I	C	G	Q	D	H	J	K	A	X
A	C	I	R	M	L	O	F	P	Z	B
N	B	N	F	E	J	W	U	L	H	F
A	Q	N	H	C	A	Y	E	G	I	L
N	D	A	Y	F	Z	M	B	K	H	O
A	Z	M	I	X	E	R	T	U	P	U
I	D	O	V	H	G	I	N	G	E	R
G	E	N	A	M	T	S	F	J	K	X
Z	H	S	U	G	A	R	B	H	W	T
B	Y	W	I	P	E	A	N	U	T	S
S	P	A	G	H	E	T	T	I	E	D

Have you read all these **Julian and Huey** stories?